Harry Potter™

ALL ABOUT THE
HOGWARTS™
HOUSES

Scholastic Inc.

ISBN 978-1-338-82815-3

10 9 8 7 6 5 4 3 2 1   22 23 24 25 26
Printed in the U.S.A.   40

First edition 2022

Scholastic Inc., 557 Broadway,
New York, NY 10012

Scholastic UK Ltd., Euston House,
24 Eversholt Street, London NW1 1DB

Scholastic Ltd., Unit 89E Lagan Road,
Dublin Industrial Estate, Glasnevin, Dublin 11

PO# 5074630 03/22

By Vanessa Moody
Select illustrations by Violet Tobacco
Book design by Jessica Meltzer

Hogwarts School of Witchcraft and Wizardry is home to four houses. Each house is named after its founder.

The four houses at Hogwarts are Gryffindor, Hufflepuff, Ravenclaw, and Slytherin. Using the grid below, draw your own Hogwarts crest.

The four founders of Hogwarts each wanted to sort different types of students into their houses. Match each founder's name with the trait their house is best known for.

GODRIC
GRYFFINDOR

WISDOM

SALAZAR
SLYTHERIN

LOYALTY

HELGA
HUFFLEPUFF

BRAVERY

ROWENA
RAVENCLAW

CUNNING

Gryffindor attracts students who are brave, courageous, and determined.

Write about a time when each of these Gryffindors showed courage!

Ginny Weasley was brave when

_____

_____

_____

_____

_____

_____

Hermione Granger was brave when

_____

_____

_____

_____

_____

_____

Dean Thomas was brave when

_____

_____

_____

_____

_____

_____

Hufflepuff attracts students who are loyal, patient, and dedicated.

Unscramble these letters to find the names of three Hufflepuff students.

CIECDR GOGYRID

_ _ _ _ _ _

_ _ _ _ _ _ _

NHANAH TBATBO

_ _ _ _ _ _

_ _ _ _ _ _

NUJSTI
ICHFN-YELFETCHL

_ _ _ _ _ _

_ _ _ _ _-

_ _ _ _ _ _ _ _ _

Ravenclaw attracts students who are wise, witty, and value education.

Fill in the blanks to spell the names of two Ravenclaw students.

C _ _

CH _ N _

L _ N _

L _ _ E G _ O _

Slytherin attracts students who are ambitious, cunning, and full of pride.

Write about a time when each of these Slytherins made sure they got their way!

Draco Malfoy

_____
_____
_____
_____
_____
_____

Pansy Parkinson

_____
_____
_____
_____
_____
_____

Crabbe and Goyle

_____
_____
_____
_____
_____
_____

As Professor McGonagall says before the Sorting Ceremony, **"Now, while you're here, your house will be like your family."**

The Sorting Hat sorts each student into their Hogwarts house. The Sorting Hat used to belong to Godric Gryffindor. Using the grid, draw your own Sorting Hat in the space below.

Sometimes, the Sorting Hat knows right away which house a student belongs to. The hat doesn't even touch Draco's head before it shouts, **"Slytherin!"**

Other times, the Sorting Hat takes longer to decide. The hat has to think for a moment before it tells Hermione she belongs in Gryffindor!

Everybody has a little bit of each house inside them. That's what makes the Sorting Hat's job so hard!

"Hmm, difficult. Very difficult," the Sorting Hat says when Harry puts it on his head. **"But where to put you?"**

Harry is sorted into Gryffindor! Can you remember times when Harry showed he was brave? What about times when he was like the students in the other houses too?

Harry was brave when

_____

_____

_____

_____

Harry was wise when

_____

_____

_____

_____

Harry was ambitious when

_____

_____

_____

_____

Harry was loyal when

_____

_____

_____

_____

The Sorting Hat has a lot to think about when making its decision. What would you tell the Sorting Hat about yourself?

I AM . . .

◇ smart

◇ witty

◇ a good friend

◇ eager

◇ brave

◇ focused

◇ kind

◇ serious

◇ strong

◇ ready for anything

The Sorting Hat also takes the students' wishes into account. Use this space to write about which house you would choose and why.

_____
_____
_____
_____
_____
_____
_____
_____
_____
_____
_____
_____
_____
_____
_____
_____
_____
_____
_____
_____
_____
_____
_____

Now that you have been sorted, color the scarf below with your new house colors!

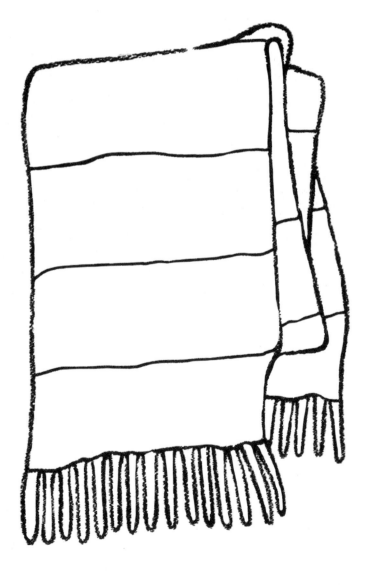

Once the first-year students are sorted, they join their house table for the feast. Everyone cheers to welcome them! Decorate this page with stickers to show all the yummy foods at the feast.

Some families in the wizarding world have many members who are all in the same house, like the Weasleys.

Ron, Ginny, and their five older brothers, Bill, Charlie, Percy, Fred, and George, are all in Gryffindor.

But siblings aren't always sorted into the same house. Sirius Black was in Gryffindor during his time at Hogwarts. His brother, Regulus, was in Slytherin.

What houses do you think you and your family would be in if you went to Hogwarts? Would you all be together or spread out across the four houses? Sort some of your family members in the spaces below.

1. _____

2. _____

3. _____

4. _____

5. _____

6. _____

Every year, students in the four houses compete to win the House Cup. They try to earn as many house points as possible — and try not to lose any too! Using the grid below, draw your own House Cup.

Hourglasses in the Great Hall keep track of the house points using colorful jewels in the house colors. Fill in the hourglasses to show which house is winning the House Cup!

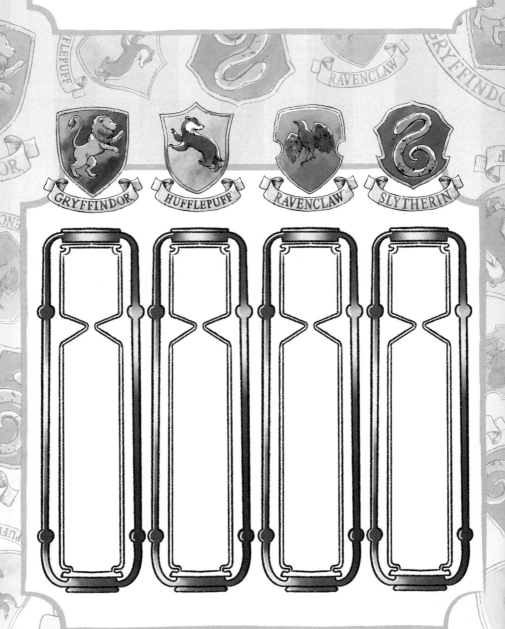

GRYFFINDOR   HUFFLEPUFF   RAVENCLAW   SLYTHERIN

Professors can give students points for good work in class or kind behavior in the halls. Match each item to its class subject to earn points for your house!

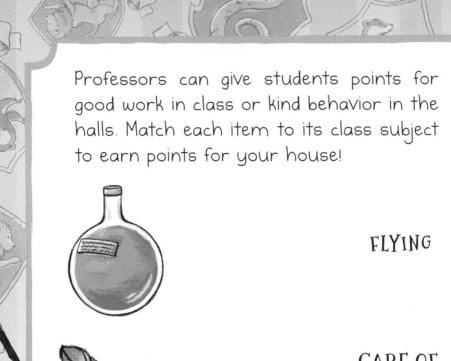

FLYING

CARE OF MAGICAL CREATURES

CHARMS

POTIONS

Professors can also take away points from a house when students don't follow the rules. Color in Neville's Remembrall below so you remember to stay on your best behavior!

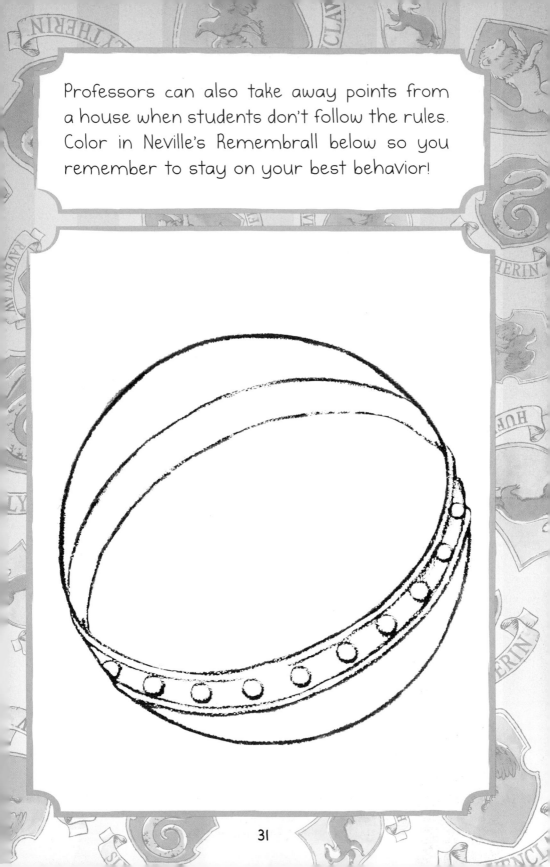

A professor can give or take away as many points as they want. Professor McGonagall takes five points from Gryffindor when Hermione says she went looking for the troll on Halloween during her first year at Hogwarts.

Then Professor McGonagall takes *fifty* points each from Harry, Hermione, Ron, and Draco for walking around the school at night. She gives them detention in the Forbidden Forest too!

Each house has older students who help the younger students in their house. These students are called prefects. Prefects can also take away house points. Ron's older brother Percy is very proud to be a prefect!

Each house has its own Quidditch team. Students can earn house points by winning their Quidditch matches. Find and circle the Snitch to win 150 points and end the game!

At the end-of-term feast, the house with the most points wins the House Cup. The Great Hall is decorated with that house's colors. Decorate the banners above to show your house has won!

Students spend a lot of time with the members of their Hogwarts house. Each house has its own common room, its own table in the Great Hall, and its own class schedules.

Students from the same house live together for all seven years at Hogwarts. Harry, Ron, Neville, Dean, and Seamus were roommates in Gryffindor Tower.

Hogwarts students also make friends with people from other houses. If you were at Hogwarts, what house do you think your best friend would belong to? Decorate these pages by drawing and using stickers to celebrate your friend's house—and yours!

My house is _____

My friend's house is _____

The people in your Hogwarts house are like a family. Your house sticks together no matter what!

Every student who has ever gone through Hogwarts's doors has been sorted into one of the four houses. Their time at Hogwarts helped them all become powerful witches and wizards!

CHO CHANG'S PATRONUS

When Mrs. Weasley was at Hogwarts, she was a determined Gryffindor! She does whatever it takes to protect the people she loves. Add arrows to her magic clock to show what each member of the Weasley family is doing.

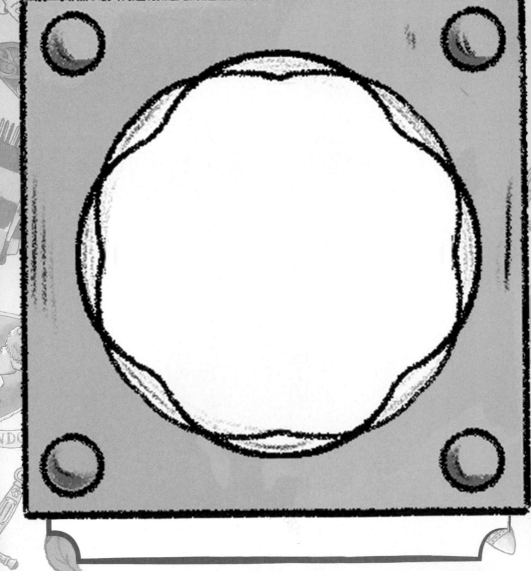

Nymphadora Tonks is an Auror and a dedicated Hufflepuff! Tonks also has a special ability. She is a Metamorphmagus. That means she can change her looks. She uses this skill to go undercover for the Order of the Phoenix. Give Tonks a fun new hair color below.

Mr. Ollivander is a wandmaker—and a wise Ravenclaw! He can match any witch or wizard with the wand that is right for them. Draw sparks around the tip of the wand you would choose in his shop.

Professor Slughorn teaches Potions and was Head of Slytherin house. He invites his favorite students to join the Slug Club. Add stickers to his cauldron to brew a potion.

GRYFFINDOR

"It takes a great deal of bravery to stand up to your enemies," says Dumbledore, "but a great deal more to stand up to your friends."

The Gryffindor colors are red and gold. Using the grid below, draw your own Gryffindor crest.

Gryffindor's symbol is a lion. When Luna wants to support the Gryffindor Quidditch team, she wears a giant lion hat that roars!

Professor McGonagall is the Head of Gryffindor house. She can be strict, but she is always very proud of her students.

Professor McGonagall teaches Transfiguration at Hogwarts. She is also an Animagus. That means she can turn into an animal at will. Professor McGonagall transforms into a cat!

If you could transform into an animal, which would you choose? Why?

_____

_____

_____

_____

_____

_____

_____

_____

_____

_____

_____

_____

_____

_____

_____

_____

_____

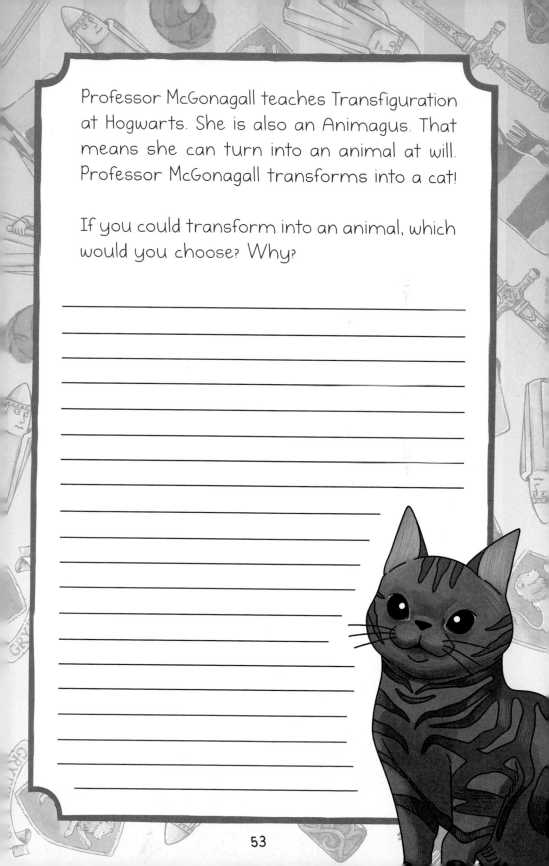

Nearly Headless Nick is the Gryffindor house ghost. He has lived at Hogwarts for over five hundred years!

The Gryffindor dormitory is located in one of Hogwarts's towers. Can you name ten Gryffindors Harry might see in the common room? (Hint: Think of the Weasleys!)

1. _____

2. _____

3. _____

4. _____

5. _____

6. _____

7. _____

8. _____

9. _____

10. _____

Each house's dormitory has a secret entrance. Gryffindor's common room is guarded by the Fat Lady. She is a portrait who loves to sing opera. The Fat Lady asks students for the password before letting them inside.

Some of the passwords used to enter the Gryffindor common room are *Caput Draconis* and *fortuna major*. Make up your own list of passwords and write them below. Don't let anyone from another house see them!

1. _____

2. _____

3. _____

4. _____

5. _____

6. _____

7. _____

8. _____

9. _____

10. _____

The Sword of Gryffindor is a magical object that once belonged to Godric Gryffindor. Using the grid, draw your own Sword of Gryffindor below.

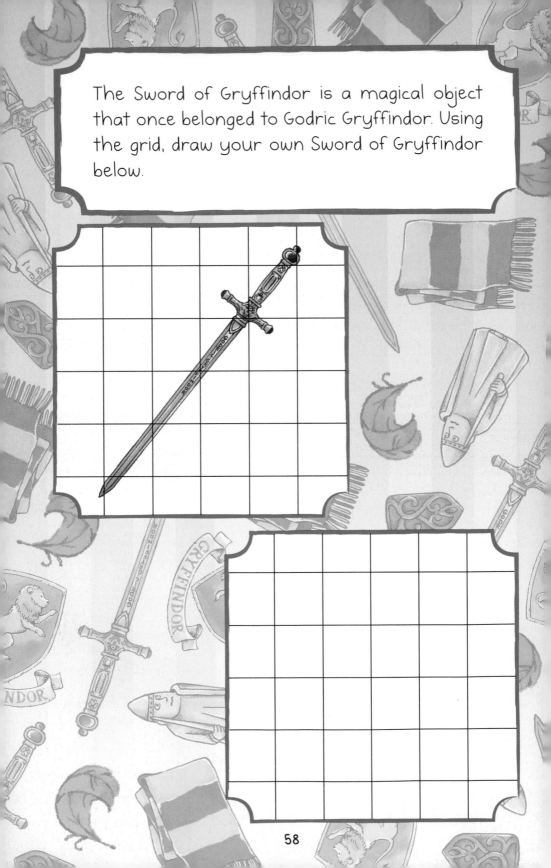

The Sword of Gryffindor can appear to worthy Gryffindors when it is needed. The sword appears to Harry when he is in the Chamber of Secrets. It appears to Neville during the Battle of Hogwarts.

Many of Harry's favorite professors are Gryffindors, just like him. Hagrid, Professor Dumbledore, and Professor McGonagall are all Gryffindors.

Professor Dumbledore gave ten points to Neville at the end of his first year at Hogwarts for standing up to his friends. Gryffindor won the House Cup! Use your stickers to give Neville the House Cup.

Most of the Weasley siblings play for the Gryffindor Quidditch team during their time at Hogwarts. Match each Weasley to their position on the Gryffindor house team on the next page.

CHASER   GEORGE

BEATER   RON

KEEPER   GINNY

BEATER   FRED

Professor Dumbledore calls Cedric Diggory hardworking, fair-minded, and a fierce friend. These traits make him a Hufflepuff.

The Hufflepuff colors are yellow and black. Using the grid below, draw your own Hufflepuff crest.

Hufflepuff's symbol is a badger. Badgers are hard workers, just like the students in Hufflepuff house. Can you think of other animals who might fit on the Hufflepuff crest? List them here!

1. _____

2. _____

3. _____

4. _____

5. _____

6. _____

7. _____

8. _____

9. _____

1º. _____

Professor Sprout teaches Herbology and is the Head of Hufflepuff house. She is supportive and kind toward all her students.

Professor Sprout helps Hogwarts students grow Mandrakes. Mandrakes have a very loud cry! Connect the dots to create earmuffs for Professor Sprout's class.

The Hufflepuff common room is near the kitchens. Color these yummy foods from the wizarding world.

Harry has many friends in Hufflepuff house, including Justin Finch-Fletchley. In his second year, Harry stops a snake from attacking Justin by speaking Parseltongue.

The house's founder, Helga Hufflepuff, had a very special cup. Using the grid, draw your own Hufflepuff cup.

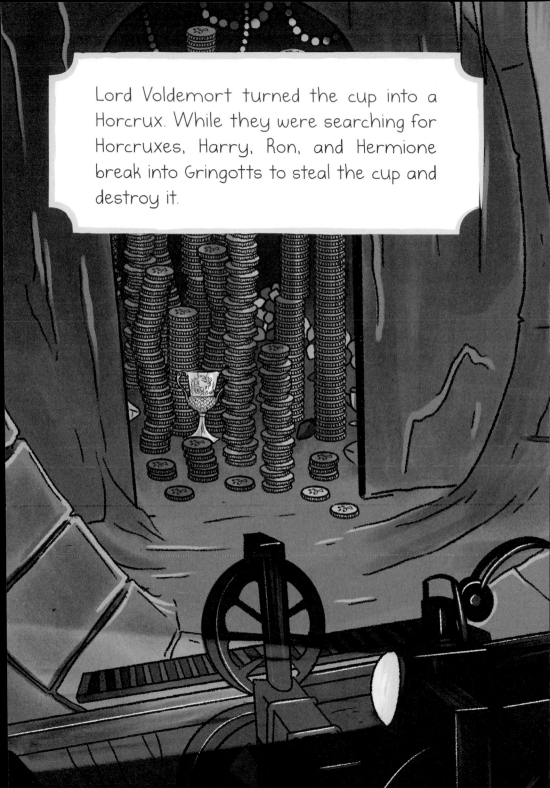

Lord Voldemort turned the cup into a Horcrux. While they were searching for Horcruxes, Harry, Ron, and Hermione break into Gringotts to steal the cup and destroy it.

Nymphadora Tonks was a Hufflepuff when she went to Hogwarts. She joins the Order of the Phoenix to help defeat Lord Voldemort. Draw a fun nose shape for Tonks to use the next time she goes undercover!

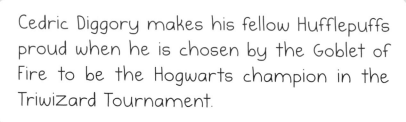

Cedric Diggory makes his fellow Hufflepuffs proud when he is chosen by the Goblet of Fire to be the Hogwarts champion in the Triwizard Tournament.

RAVENCLAW

"Wit beyond measure is man's greatest treasure," said Rowena Ravenclaw.

The Ravenclaw colors are blue and silver. Using the grid, draw your own Ravenclaw crest.

The Ravenclaw symbol is a bird, of course! So many kinds of birds are smart—just like the members of Ravenclaw house.

Professor Flitwick is the Head of Ravenclaw house. He also teaches Charms and is a dueling champion.

The Ravenclaw house ghost is the Gray Lady. She helps Harry find Rowena Ravenclaw's lost diadem during the Battle of Hogwarts.

Ravenclaw's diadem was also turned into a Horcrux by Lord Voldemort. Harry knows it is hidden in the Room of Requirement—but where? Can you find the diadem for Harry?

Ravenclaw's dormitory is at the top of a tall tower. Students have to solve a riddle to enter the common room. Can you answer this riddle? Draw your guess below!

What has many, many holes but can still hold water?

Ravenclaws are known for being smart. But Ravenclaws are wise in many different ways. Luna Lovegood is known for her creativity.

Cho Chang is a fast learner. She uses her wits when learning new spells and charms as part of Dumbledore's Army.

Other Ravenclaw students love thinking about the unknown in Divination class with fellow Ravenclaw Professor Trelawney.

The Sorting Hat tells new students that being chosen for Slytherin house could help them on their way to greatness.

The Slytherin colors are green and silver. Using the grid below, draw your own Slytherin crest.

Slytherin's symbol is a snake. Salazar Slytherin was a Parseltongue, which means he could talk to snakes. Harry and Voldemort can both talk to snakes too!

Professor Snape is the Head of Slytherin house. He teaches Potions, and his lessons can be very hard.

When Professor Snape becomes Hogwarts headmaster, Professor Slughorn takes his place as Head of Slytherin house.

Students need a password to enter the Slytherin dormitory, just like they do in the other houses. Come up with a few ideas for your own Slytherin passwords and write them below. Don't show them to anyone else!

1. _____

2. _____

3. _____

4. _____

5. _____

6. _____

7. _____

8. _____

9. _____

10. _____

The Slytherin dormitory is located in the dungeons. Harry and Ron visit the Slytherin common room in their second year by disguising themselves with Polyjuice Potion. But first they have to get Crabbe and Goyle out of the way! Connect the dots to sneak into the common room with this Sleeping Draught cupcake.

Draco Malfoy is the Seeker for Slytherin's Quidditch team. Draw a Snitch for Draco to find.

In his second year, Draco's father buys Nimbus 2001 broomsticks for the Slytherin Quidditch team. The team is more interested in winning than following the Quidditch rules.

Slytherin won the House Cup many years in a row before Harry was a student at Hogwarts! Color the House Cup below green to celebrate Slytherin's winning streak. Don't forget to write the house name on the plaque.

Long ago, Salazar Slytherin created a hidden part of Hogwarts castle. He called it the Chamber of Secrets. Harry discovers the Chamber in the girls' bathroom.

Do you have a secret hiding spot? Where is it? What do you do there? If you don't have one, imagine what your secret hiding spot might be like in the space below!

_____

_____

_____

_____

_____

_____

_____

_____

_____

_____

_____

_____

_____

_____

_____

_____

_____

_____

"There's not a witch or wizard who went bad who wasn't in Slytherin," says Ron.

But not all Dark wizards come from Slytherin house. Peter Pettigrew was in Gryffindor when he was in school. And Professor Quirrell was in Ravenclaw.

Many students feel pride about belonging to their Hogwarts house. And they make many friends there too!

Do you belong to a group that you are proud to be a part of? It could be a club, a sports team, a band, or the cast of a play. Write all about it here. Include why you are proud to be in this group and all about the friends you've made there!

_____

_____

_____

_____

_____

_____

_____

_____

_____

_____

_____

_____

_____

_____

_____

_____

_____

_____

_____

_____

_____

"It is not our abilities that show what we truly are. It is our choices," says Professor Dumbledore. Place stickers inside the heart that represent the kinds of choices you like to make.

Just remember, students who are brave and cunning and loyal and wise are found in every house at Hogwarts.

Can you remember a time that you showed your Gryffindor side?

_____
_____
_____
_____
_____
_____
_____
_____
_____

What about your inner Hufflepuff?

_____
_____
_____
_____
_____
_____
_____
_____
_____

When did your Ravenclaw spirit come out?

_____

_____

_____

_____

_____

_____

_____

_____

_____

_____

Have you had any Slytherin moments?

_____

_____

_____

_____

_____

_____

_____

_____

_____

_____

_____

You don't need to be in Hufflepuff to be a hard worker.

You don't need to be in Slytherin to be resourceful.

And you don't need to be in Ravenclaw to be smart.

You only need to be yourself. No matter where the Sorting Hat sorts you, you will always have a home at Hogwarts.